ROODICA THE RUDE

and the Famous Flea Trick

CATNIP BOOKS
Published by Catnip Publishing Ltd.
14 Greville Street
London EC1N 8SB

First published 2009
1 3 5 7 9 10 8 6 4 2

Text copyright © Margaret Ryan, 2009
Illustrations copyright © Sarah Horne, 2009
The moral rights of the author and illustrator have been asserted

All rights reserved

A CIP catalogue record for this book is available from the British Library

ISBN 978-1-84647-072-1

Printed in Poland

www.catnippublishing.co.uk

ROODICA THE RUDE

and the Famous Flea Trick

MARGARET RYAN

Catnip

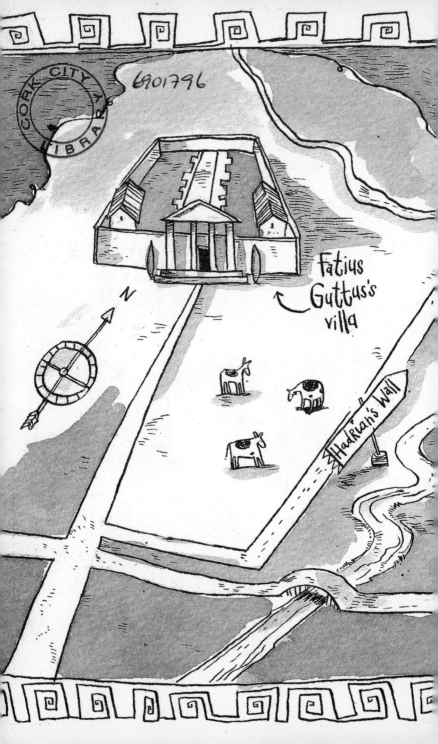

CORK CITY LIBRARY

6901796

Fatius Guttus's villa

N

Hadrian's Wall

For Philippa Milnes-Smith

Roodica's Royals (The Celts)

KING BREN

King of Brensland

Likes fighting, fighting and fighting. Oh, and wars, where he's usually to be found, right in the middle of the fighting.

QUEEN GOODICA

Queen of Brensland

Likes peace and quiet. Lives at Maiden Castle trying to bring up her three daughters as proper princesses.

PRINCESS FOODICA

Princess Foodica

The eldest daughter and a proper princess. She's always neat and tidy, never says anything wrong, and is a wonderful cook.

9

Princess Woodica

The middle daughter and
a proper Princess. She's always
sweet and gentle, never does
anything wrong, and makes
wonderful things out of wood.

Princess Roodica

The youngest daughter and a proper...pain in
the posterior. She's never neat and tidy, never
sweet and gentle, and is
always saying and doing
everything wrong. Her
mother wonders what on
earth she'll do with her.

Roodica's Friends
Fleabag, the wolfhound
He goes everywhere
with Roodica.

Plodette, the pony
She carries Roodica
around sometimes.
Slowly.

Gideon, the horse boy
He tries to keep Roodica
out of trouble.
Fat chance!

The Terrible Togas (The Romans)

Magnus Maximus (Big Max)

Very superstitious Roman
Governor. Likes ordering
people about and getting
presents. Wishes someone would
hurry up and invent underpants
as he finds Britain rather chilly.

Fatius Guttus (Fat Gut)

Tax Collector (Boo Hisssss).
Likes collecting taxes, taxes,
and more taxes, especially
from those crummy Celts.
Also likes eating, drinking
and burping loudly.

Copius Mucus (Lottasnot)

Son of Fatius Guttus.
Likes telling tales,
sneaking up
on people
and sniffing.

COPIUS MUCUS

Roman Alert!

It was late morning and the sun shone brightly on the thatched roof of Maiden Castle. Inside, nearly everyone was busy. Princess Foodica was busy adding wild herbs to the stew bubbling in the bronze pot on the open fire.

"That stew smells delicious, Foodica," said Queen Goodica, "and will taste even better, I'm sure. I don't know what we'd do without you."

17

Foodica gave her mother a gentle smile and stirred the stew with a long wooden spoon.

Princess Woodica was busy carving a little mouse on the back of a chair she had just made.

"That looks splendid, Woodica," said her mother. "Farmer Ned has promised me lots of wool in exchange for that chair. With it I'll be able to weave some warm winter cloaks for the settlement children. I don't know what we'd do without you."

Woodica smiled happily and chipped the last splinter off the mouse's tail. Princess Roodica, busy doing nothing, caught the splinter and picked her teeth with it.

"DON'T DO THAT **ROODICA!**"

said her mother.
Roodica huffed, screwed up her freckly
nose and pulled a strand of curly red
hair down into a pretend moustache.

19

Roodica made her favourite exploding duck noise. Her dog, Fleabag, who was used to it, just blinked his big brown eyes and twitched his black nose, but the ducks, snoozing outside in the old chariot, quacked in alarm.

"I'm bored," muttered Roodica, stroking Fleabag's floppy ears.

"Then find something to do," said the queen, picking up her sewing. "Princesses should always be busy."

"Okay," grinned Roodica, and started to catch the fleas that leapt off Fleabag.

"Gotcha!" she said. "That's the tenth one today."

21

Fleabag woofed happily and thumped his tail, but the queen shook her royal head and shuddered. "You're not a bit like a proper princess, Roodica. Not neat. Not clean. And certainly not tidy. I'm afraid you take after your father's side of the family. What am I going to do with you?"

"You could always send me off to find Father," suggested Roodica, not in the least put out. "I could help him fight the hairy painted Picts. I could take Fleabag and Gideon and we could hitch Plodette up to the old chariot. It would be far better than hanging around here having to be nice to the rotten Romans all the time. Why did they have to come

here anyway? Why couldn't they stay in their own country? Why couldn't they mind their own business? Why....?"

"Hush," said the queen. "You ask too many questions. The Romans are here, and, for safety's sake, we must try not to annoy them."

"You're far too nice," snorted Roodica. "I know what I'd like to do to them. I'd like to get Will, the blacksmith, to make me a BIG sword with a really, really sharp point. I'd heave it up and twirl it round and round my head then stick it in their…"

"ROODICA!"

"Remember you're a princess!"

"Sorry," muttered Roodica.

But she wasn't.

She was sorry, though, to hear the rumble of wheels and see the approach of a fast chariot. She jumped up, startling Fleabag and his fleas.

25

"ROMAN ALERT!"
"ROMAN ALERT!"

"Here come two of the terrible togas now!" cried Roodica.

"Which two?" asked her mother.

"Fatius Guttus and Copius Mucus."

"Quick!" cried Foodica. "Hide the stew."

"Quick!" cried Woodica, "Hide the chair."

But it was too late.

26

A Brilliant Idea!

Fatius Guttus, the tax collector, and his snivelling son, Copius Mucus, drew up to the castle in their fine chariot, which was drawn by a beautiful golden mare.

Fatius stepped down, adjusted his white toga and checked that the hefty money pouch on his belt was secure. Copius stepped down and sneezed loudly, hands on hips.

Roodica stood at the castle doorway, "We're not in," she shouted. "Go away."

The Romans ignored her and went inside.

"Salve! Greetings, Queen Goodica," wheezed Fatius. "Copius and I were passing and thought we would make sure that you were well."

"We're fine," said Roodica. "Now buzz off."

"Roodica, please don't be rude. Fatius, do sit down and take the weight off your…"

"Stomach?" suggested Roodica.

"Feet," said her mother. "Would you like some water to quench your thirst?"

"Have you no beer?" asked Fatius,

running his fat sausage fingers over the little mouse on the back of the new chair, before lowering his vast behind into it.

CORK CITY LIBRARY

"You drank it all last time you were here, Guzzleguts," muttered Roodica.

"I bet you've hidden it somewhere," sneered Copius. "You Celts are always hiding things to avoid paying taxes." And he began rummaging inside the

royal storage chests. "Huh, just old skins and blankets," he said, casting them on the floor, and kicking them with his sandalled foot.

"Leave those alone, Lottasnot, or I'll set Fleabag on you," hissed Roodica.

"Hah! Fat chance," smirked Copius,

"My dog Brutus, is far fiercer than your stupid wolfhound," and he began to clatter around among Foodica's cooking pots. "As I thought," he cried, holding up a beaker, "Beer!"

"It's only a little flat stuff I was saving to flavour some boiled beef," whispered Foodica.

"What's that I smell cooking at the moment?" asked Copius, his large, red veined nose quivering.

"Just a little mutton stew. Not worthy of you at all," said Foodica.

"Nonsense, girl. You could make a soldier's sandal taste good and mutton

stew's my favourite. We'll stay to lunch."
"Certainly," said the queen politely. "I'm
sure there's enough for everyone."
Roodica scowled as Woodica set out five
wooden platters and spoons on the long
table, whilst Foodica collected some
wooden bowls.

"Serve our guests first,
Foodica," instructed
the queen.
"Yes, Mother,"
said Foodica,
and began
to ladle out
the stew.
Fatius watched
her hungrily.

"That's not nearly enough, girl. Fill my bowl right up. I'm a grown man, you know."

"And growing bigger by the minute," muttered Roodica.

"And I'm a growing boy. Fill mine right up, too," ordered Copius.

"Very well," said Foodica. But, by the time she had filled up their two bowls, there was no stew left for the others. Fatius and Copius didn't care. They set about slurping the stew; shovelling it into their cavernous mouths as fast as they could.

"Where's the bread?" whined Copius. "We must have bread with our stew. Don't you Celts know anything?"

"I'll get it," offered Roodica, and was about to bounce the crusty roll on Copius's head, when her mother shot her a warning look. She placed it on his wooden platter instead, and, with a pretend smile, hissed in his ear. "I hope it chokes you, and you turn purple, swell up and burst, you slimy little toad!"

But Copius just smiled nastily and stuffed a large lump into his mouth. "This bread and stew are delicious," he smirked, spitting bits everywhere. "What a pity there's none left for you."

"That certainly was an excellent lunch," Fatius sat back in the new chair, patted his fat belly and burped.

"I get a row for doing that," muttered Roodica, "and for wiping my nose on my sleeve," she added, catching Copius in the act.

"Well," said Fatius, easing himself up. "Time to drive back to our villa for a nap. Always best after a large lunch, don't you think." Then he ran his hand over the back of the chair and stroked the little carved mouse again. "I'll take this chair with me, if you don't mind. I'm expecting Magnus Maximus, the governor, this afternoon and this will look well in my new bath house."

"Yes, we do mind actually!" yelled Roodica. "That chair's not for us, it's for ..."

"Hush, Roodica," said her mother. "Take the chair if you wish, Fatius, we are pleased you admire it."

And the queen stood by, quietly dignified,

while Fatius and Copius removed the
chair then drove off in their
chariot, scattering ducks
as they went.
Woodica burst into tears.
"Now we've no
chair to exchange
for the wool.
Now the
children won't
get their winter
cloaks. Now
they'll be
so cold."

Foodica burst into tears.

"We've no lunch and the stew was to be a special treat for us."

"I know, girls," sighed the queen, "but with your father away, we just have to put up with it. If we upset the Romans they might turn us out of our home, or worse still, take it out on the people of the settlement. There's nothing we can do."

"Nothing," sniffed Foodica.

"Absolutely nothing," sniffed Woodica.

"Rubbish," muttered Roodica. "I'm not going to let the rotten Romans get away with it. It's just not fair. The children need these cloaks. Come on, Fleabag, let's find Gideon. I have a brilliant idea."

Has Anyone seen Gideon?

Roodica and Fleabag left Maiden Castle to look for Gideon.

"I don't know where he'll be today," Roodica told Fleabag. "We'll just have to look around the settlement. Let's try Will's place first."

The two of them headed downhill towards the blacksmith's.

"Hi, Roodica," called one of the local children, as they passed by.

"Want to join my team for a game of kick the apple?"

"Okay. Just a very quick game," said Roodica. She hitched up her skirts and pitched into the game, kicking and dribbling and passing the battered and bruised apple, till her team was level with the other team 2-2. Then Fleabag got hold of the apple and ate it.

"Sorry, guys," apologised Roodica. "I'll

pinch one for you from Foodica's apple loft later, but right now I must go to the blacksmith's. Bye."

When Roodica and Fleabag got to the forge they found Will, his forehead shining with beads of sweat, hammering a hoe into shape. "Hullo, Will," shouted Roodica above the din. "I'm looking for Gideon. Have you seen him?"

"Nope," Will shook his shaggy head.

"And don't come near me with that lousy dog. Makes me itch just to look at him. Try Sam's place."

"Oh look, now you've hurt Fleabag's feelings, Will," grinned Roodica, as the dog gave himself an almighty shake and dislodged a whole family of fleas.

"Come on, Fleabag. Race you to Sadler Sam's."

Fleabag easily got there first, and Roodica arrived just in time to see him put his big paws on Sam's shoulders and topple him over onto a pile of saddles.

Then he licked Sam's face all over.

"Get this flea-bitten hound off me," yelled Sam. "He smells terrible."

"Nearly as bad as you, Sam,"

grinned Roodica.
"But at least your
face is clean now.
We're really looking
for Gideon. Have
you seen him?"
Sam got up and
scratched himself
furiously.
"No. Why don't you go
and ask old Mother Silverlocks.
She's the wise woman. She's supposed
to know everything that goes on
around here."
"Good idea." grinned Roodica, "Let's go,
Fleabag." And they ran down the hill and
out of the stockade.

Roodica waved to Little Joe, the herdsman, guarding the grazing cattle, then turned towards the forest and the cave of Old Mother Silverlocks.

Roodica and Fleabag went deep into the forest to where the trees grew dense and the light grew dim. Fleabag stayed close to Roodica, sniffing the air and listening for danger.

He stopped dead in his tracks and his hackles rose when a cracked voice rang out…

**" Who dares come this way?
Who dares disturb my day?"**

But Roodica just grinned. "Why do you have to ask, Mother Silverlocks? I thought you were supposed to know everything around here."

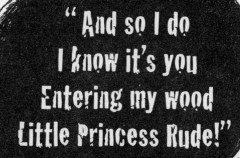

"And so I do
I know it's you
Entering my wood
Little Princess Rude!"

"You know I'm looking for Gideon then."
Old Mother Silverlocks emerged from her
cave which was hidden behind some trees.
The wise woman was small and thin with
stick-like arms and legs, and wore a black
tunic and cloak. She pointed a long
skinny finger at Roodica.

"I know what I know,
I know, of course,
You'll find boy Gideon
With a horse."

"You're right," cried Roodica. "Why didn't I think of that? Gideon was helping to erect a fence yesterday. He'll be in the new pen with the horses."

"He **IS** the horse boy. Try using your brains for a change," cackled Old Mother Silverlocks.

But Roodica and Fleabag were already hurrying away and didn't hear.

When they got back to the settlement they found Gideon in the pen patiently trying to get a bridle over the head of a very lively pony.

"Hi Giddy-Up," yelled Roodica, jumping up onto the barred gate.

"Stop what you're doing

RIGHT NOW, I need you."

The pony's eyes grew wild, and he reared and knocked Gideon over, before bolting to the far side of the pen. Gideon scowled at Roodica, got up, and dusted down his tunic and leggings. "How often have I told you not to yell near the horses, you nitwit. It'll take me ages to get near Frisky again."

"Sorry," muttered Roodica. "Forgot. But this is important. I really need you to do something for me."

Gideon vaulted over the gate. "I don't care if you are a princess," he said. "I'm not doing your homework again."

"Too right you're not, you stupid idiot," snorted Roodica. "You got it all correct last time, so Druid Big Brain knew I hadn't done it. Now I've got extra to do for next week."

"And I'm not practising javelin throwing in the forest again either. I've still got the bruises from last time."

"If you will crawl around searching for your stick with your bum in the air…" grinned Roodica. "I thought you were a wild boar. Anyway it's nothing as dangerous as that. Fatius and Copius have just been to Maiden Castle and stolen the chair we were going to exchange for the wool to make the children's winter cloaks. I have a brilliant idea to get it back, but I need your help. First of all, I need you to teach me how to drive the old chariot."

So it was Gideon's turn to look thoughtful.

Teach *you* to drive the old chariot? And you think that's not dangerous?

It won't be if we patch the old chariot up first. I know it's falling apart in places, and is full of feathers and duck poo, but...

That's not
what's dangerous.
You driving it is what's
dangerous. You don't know
your left from your right or
your up from your down.
And you've no idea what the
word STOP means.
I am not going to teach
you to drive. **No way.**
No chance.

I could ask
Foodica to make
you some of her
special pancakes.
They're your
very favourite…

54

Well...I don't know...

With lots of her creamy butter that's your very, very favourite...

Well I…

"Good. That's settled then," said Roodica. "We'll repair the chariot and put a harness on Plodette. Come on, Gideon, there's no time to lose."

Driving Lessons

Gideon shooed the ducks out of the chariot then began to repair it with some wood and iron nails. Roodica and Fleabag meantime, hurried to the field behind Maiden Castle to fetch Plodette. "Hi, Plodette," called Roodica sweetly. "How would you like to go for a gallop?"

Plodette snorted and carried on cropping the sweet grass.

"Come on, Plodette," urged Roodica, stroking her nose. "It'll be fun." Plodette ignored her.

"Hmm," said Roodica, and went round to the back end to try to push her piebald pony out of the field.

Plodette swished her tail in Roodica's face, dug her hooves in, and wouldn't budge.

Roodica thought for a moment then ran back to the castle. Her mother and sisters were out so no one saw her climb the ladder into the apple loft. "Foodica won't miss a couple of these," she decided, and hurried back to the field with two juicy, red apples.

She waved the apples under Plodette's nose. The pony gave a greedy whinny. Roodica walked backwards holding out the apples. Plodette followed. Eventually Roodica managed to lead her to where the old chariot was waiting, and Plodette finally got her reward.

Gideon hammered the last nail into the old chariot and Fleabag went to inspect his work.

"It's not great," Gideon said, running his hands through his thick black hair, "But it'll have to do." He harnessed Plodette to the chariot, but, despite his soothing words, she wasn't best pleased.

"Let's go Plodette"

She was even less pleased when Roodica jumped into the chariot, picked up the reins and yelled.

Gideon sighed and shook his head. "I knew this was a bad idea. You have to take it slowly, Roodica. Give a little tug on both reins and make a clicking noise with your tongue. That way Plodette will know you want to set off."

"Okay," said Roodica. She shook the reins and clucked like a noisy farmyard chicken. Fleabag looked puzzled. Plodette didn't move.

"The horse is deaf," decided Roodica. "Perhaps I should yell in her ear." Gideon shook his head, took the reins from her, and clicked his tongue. They set off. "Now you take the reins, Roodica, and just keep going forwards .... slowly."

"Hey," grinned Roodica, after they had bumped along gently for a few minutes, "I'm a natural chariot driver. This is really easy."

"Okay," said Gideon. "Now we need to turn right."

"Why?" asked Roodica. "I like going straight on."

"There's a barn in the way."

"So there is. Who put that there?"

"Tug gently on the right rein."

"Okay."

"Your other right," yelled Gideon.

"Whee," said Roodica, as they tore off

the barn's
open door,
"This is fun!"
Gideon let out
a long breath.

"Remind me to write L and R on the
back of your hands," he muttered.

"You make such a fuss," said Roodica.
"What's next?"

"Turn left before we hit the oak tree."

"Left? That's errm…"

"The hand nearest me."

"Oh, that left. Why didn't you say?"

But before Roodica could tug on the
rein, Plodette spotted some juicy grass
and came to a standstill.

"Okay," said Gideon, leaping out of the

chariot, and going to Plodette's head.
"This is a good time to show you how to
back up."

"That sounds boring. I don't want to back
up. I want to go forwards really, really fast
RIGHT NOW," said Roodica, and she
jerked on the reins.

Startled, Plodette took off through the
settlement at top speed. Startled, Fleabag
took off after her.

"Whee hee," cried Roodica. "I knew this would be fun!"

Plodette's hooves thundered, Fleabag's ears flapped, and Roodica's teeth rattled as they hurtled over the rough ground. Ducks squawked in alarm, dogs ran for cover, and a hay cart overturned, as Roodica flew past. She held on tightly as they swerved through the open gate of the stockade scattering the grazing cattle, before ploughing through a field of ripening barley.

Eventually, Plodette got tired and they came to an abrupt halt at the other side.

"Phew," gasped Roodica. "That was exciting."

Fleabag sat back on his haunches, his big pink tongue lolling out. This was a great new game.

A panting, red-faced Gideon finally caught up with them.

"What kept you?" grinned Roodica. "This chariot driving's fantastic. I think I'm getting the hang of it now."

"Idiot," gasped Gideon. "Move over."

And he drove the rest of the way to Fatius's villa while Roodica explained her brilliant idea.

"I want you to hide the chariot in that clump of trees close to the new bath house, Gideon," she instructed, as they drew near. "And stay with Plodette while Fleabag and I sneak over there. I don't want her wandering around giving the game away."

"I wish I was coming with you. This is a crazy idea. Be careful," whispered Gideon.

"Amn't I always careful?"

"You couldn't even spell it."

"I think Druid Big Brain would probably agree with you about that," grinned Roodica.

Big Max

Roodica and Fleabag slipped over to the new bath house and peeped over the old stone wall.

They were just in time to see Fatius show off his new bath to the Roman governor.

"Nice mosaic tiles," nodded Magnus Maximus. "But I really like this." And he ran his hand over Woodica's chair.

"Well, it was rather expensive, but I

bought the chair especially for you, Governor," beamed Fatius.

"What!" Roodica clapped her hand over her mouth.

"I love the little carved mouse," said Magnus Maximus, "and the chair is very comfortable. I think I may have a nap in it."

"By all means," said Fatius, and bowed several times as he left backwards.

"Now's our chance, Fleabag," whispered Roodica. "Where are your fleas?"

She ruffled his coat, caught several fleas, then popped them into the little leather pouch at her waist.

"That should be enough." she whispered. She peeped over the wall again.

The governor was sprawled in the chair, the laurel wreath on his head askew, and his hairy legs crossed at the ankles. He was snoring loudly. Roodica climbed over the wall, tiptoed towards him and slipped the fleas inside his toga. Then she hurried back to Fleabag and settled down to wait.

But not for long.

Soon Magnus Maximus was snoring and scratching. First his chest, then his neck, then his bald head. That wakened him up. He leapt into the air. "O me miserum! Woe is me! What's happening…" Up and down his legs and arms and all over his body he scratched. Then he began jumping around, shaking out his toga and yelling. "Get off me. Get off me, you little…"

"What's the matter, Governor? Did you have a bad dream?" cried Fatius, rushing to his side and clutching his hand. "Are you ill?" asked Copius, grabbing the other.

"Not ill. Itchy, you fools!" yelled the governor. "That chair you gave me was full of fleas!" And he took a step forward and plunged fully clad into the bath, taking Fatius and Copius with him. Fatius came up coughing and spluttering. "A a a a thousand apologies, Governor. We'll remove the chair at once. Stupid, stupid Celts!"

Copius came up sneezing.

"Aaa tishoo. Aaa tishoo."

They all waded to the side and Fatius and Copius tried to help Magnus Maximus out of the bath, but he shrugged them off angrily. "Get away from me," he said.

"I'm so sorry about the chair, Governor," said Fatius. "I had no idea…"

"You're nine kinds of an idiot, Fatius," Magnus Maximus muttered, as he wrung out his dripping toga. "Where's my laurel wreath?"

Fatius looked round and saw it floating in the bath. He pushed Copius back in to fetch it.

The governor stuck it on his bald head. Water dripped down his face. "You haven't heard the last of this, Fatius," he thundered, and stormed off, his wet toga flapping about his long legs. "Mangy, flea-ridden Celts," muttered Fatius, as he and Copius picked up the chair and threw it over the wall. From her hiding place behind a large oak, Roodica grinned, and, as soon as night fell, she crept out and lugged the chair back to where Gideon was waiting.

"My brilliant idea worked," she told him happily, as they loaded the chair onto the chariot and headed for home. When they arrived back at Maiden Castle Foodica, Woodica and the queen were pacing anxiously.

"Where have you been, Roodica?" scolded the queen. "It's very late and we've been worried."

"Just getting back some stolen property," grinned Roodica and unloaded the chair and told them what had happened.

"You should have seen Big Max doing the flea dance," she giggled, prancing about just like the governor. "And Fatius's belly was **enormous**, wobbling about in his wet toga." And she stuffed a blanket inside her tunic to show everyone.

Foodica and Woodica giggled and the queen smiled. "It was a very dangerous thing to do, Roodica, but very brave. Now the children will be warm this winter in the new cloaks I promised them."

"And Gideon will get the pancakes I promised him?"

"Of course," said Foodica. "I'll make some right away. And some for you, too. You must be hungry."

"You can eat them sitting in the little

mouse chair," grinned Woodica.

When the pancakes were ready, Gideon took his home, and Roodica sat by the open fire sharing hers with Fleabag. As usual, every time Fleabag moved, fleas jumped off him.

Roodica laughed and brushed them away. "What would we have done without your fleas, Fleabag?" she said.

Fleabag didn't reply, but the queen looked over at her youngest daughter fondly. "What would we do without *you*, Roodica?" she said.